AuthorHouse™
1663 Liberty Drive
Bloomington, IN 47403
www.authorhouse.com
Phone: 1 (800) 839-8640

Published by AuthorHouse 01/24/2019

ISBN: 978-1-5462-7643-2 (sc)
ISBN: 978-1-5462-7644-9 (e)

Library of Congress Control Number: 2019900576

Print information available on the last page.

Any people depicted in stock imagery provided by Getty Images are models,
and such images are being used for illustrative purposes only.
Certain stock imagery © Getty Images.

This book is printed on acid-free paper.

authorHOUSE®

pocket 2

Pockets noticed a little girl running so fast that she slipped on a banana peel, which injured her knee. She started crying, and so Pockets went over to her and smiled.

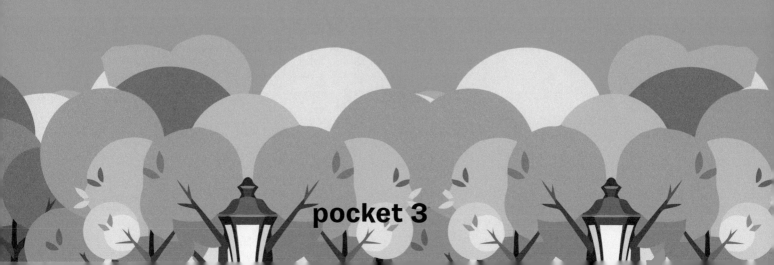

pocket 3

pocket 4

She seemed disturbed and said, "What are you smiling about? Didn't you just see me fall?"

pocket 6

He said, "I'm smiling because I saw a dinosaur on your knee."

She said, "There's no dinosaur on my knee!"

He said, "Let me see."

She showed him her knee.

pocket 8

He reached into one of his pockets and pulled out a wet tissue to clean the boo-boo. Then he reached into another pocket and pulled out a Band-Aid that had a picture of a dinosaur on it. He put it on her knee.

He said, "Look! I told you so!"

She replied, "You just put that there!"

pocket 9

pocket 10

Pockets said, "But I didn't tell you how it got there."

They both started laughing. Laughing is like good medicine.

"My pain is gone!" she said, grinning.

pocket 12

Then all of Pockets's pockets started to light up and flash and "Funky Town" started playing.

Pockets started dancing and waved goodbye.

pocket 13

pocket 14

The little girl blew a kiss to Pockets, and without looking back, Pockets caught the kiss and put it into one of his pockets.

pocket 15

The End

Draw your own pockets

Draw your own pockets

Draw your own pockets

Draw your own pockets

Draw your own pockets

Printed in the United States
By Bookmasters